# crooked

## by

## Catherine Trieschmann

A SAMUEL FRENCH ACTING EDITION

SAMUEL FRENCH

FOUNDED 1830

NEW YORK HOLLYWOOD LONDON TORONTO

SAMUELFRENCH.COM

## IMPORTANT BILLING AND CREDIT REQUIREMENTS

All producers of *CROOKED* *must* give credit to the Author of the Play in all programs distributed in connection with performances of the Play, and in all instances in which the title of the Play appears for the purposes of advertising, publicizing or otherwise exploiting the Play and/or a production. The name of the Author *must* appear on a separate line on which no other name appears, immediately following the title and *must* appear in size of type not less than fifty percent of the size of the title type.

In addition the following credit *must* be given in all programs and publicity information distributed in association with this piece:

Originally presented Off-Broadway at The Summer Play Festival
Produced in London in 2006 by the Bush Theatre
Produced in New York City in 2008 by Women's Project
Julie Crosby, Producing Artistic Director

*crooked* was first performed in a workshop production at the Edinburgh Fringe Festival in August 2004. It was directed by Elena Hartwell. Costumes designed by Donald Sanders. Sound designed by Claire Campbell. Emily Ballou was the stage manager.

LANEY . . . . . . . . . . . . . . . . . . . . . . . . . . . . . . . . . . . . . . . . . . . . Shelly Stover
ELISE . . . . . . . . . . . . . . . . . . . . . . . . . . . . . . . . . . . . . . . . . . Vanessa Shealy
MARIBEL . . . . . . . . . . . . . . . . . . . . . . . . . . . . . . . Katherine Sanderlin

*crooked* was presented as part of the Summer Play Festival in July 2005. It was directed by Linsay Firman. The set was designed by Susan Zeeman Rogers, costumes were designed by Sarah Tosetti and lights were designed by Aaron Black. Original music designed by Shane Rettig. Madelaine Hartman was the stage manager.

LANEY . . . . . . . . . . . . . . . . . . . . . . . . . . . . . . . . . . . . . . . . . . . . Shelly Stover
ELISE . . . . . . . . . . . . . . . . . . . . . . . . . . . . . . . . . . . . . . . . . . Effie Johnson
MARIBEL . . . . . . . . . . . . . . . . . . . . . . . . . . . . . . . Katherine Sanderlin

*crooked* premiered at the Bush Theatre in London in May 2006. It was directed by Mike Bradwell. Sets and costumes designed by Libbie Watson. Lights designed by James Farncombe. Julia Crammar was the stage manager.

LANEY . . . . . . . . . . . . . . . . . . . . . . . . . . . . . . . . . . . . . . . . . . . . Amanda Hale
ELISE . . . . . . . . . . . . . . . . . . . . . . . . . . . . . . . . . . . . . . . . . Suzan Sylvester
MARIBEL . . . . . . . . . . . . . . . . . . . . . . . . . . . . . . . . . . . Debbie Chazen

*crooked* premiered Off-Broadway at Women's Project in April 2008. It was directed by Liz Diamond. Set designed by Jennifer Moeller. Costumes designed by Ilona Somogyi. Lights designed by S. Ryan Schmidt. Sound and original music designed by Jane Shaw. Jack Gianino was the stage manager.

LANEY . . . . . . . . . . . . . . . . . . . . . . . . . . . . . . . . . . . . . . . . . . . . Cristin Milioti
ELISE . . . . . . . . . . . . . . . . . . . . . . . . . . . . . . . . . . . . . . . . . . Betsy Aidem
MARIBEL . . . . . . . . . . . . . . . . . . . . . . . . . . . . . . . Carmen M. Herlihy

## CHARACTERS

**LANEY WATERS** - 14, has dystonia, which causes one of her shoulders to draw up, as though she has a slightly hunched back.

**ELISE WATERS** - 40s, Laney's mother

**MARIBEL PURDY** - 16, Laney's friend, chubby and radiant

## PLACE

Oxford, Mississippi

## SETTING

The Water's House - Living Room, Porch
High School Stadium Bleachers
Church Sanctuary

## TIME

The Present

*For my mother, Donna*

*Special thanks to Elsa Neuwald, Mike Bradwell, Arielle Tepper, Julie Crosby, Dan Kois, V. Jane Windsor and the Waterside Seven Writer's Group, especially Gwydion Suilebhan and Mary Lane.*

## Scene One

*(**LANEY** reads her story to the audience.)*

**LANEY.** Ernest's hands smelled like lemons and gunshot. Every Monday, he parked his lemonade stand at the entrance of the park, where it stood solid as a bank. He liked the feel of the sun on his back, hot and burning like an open sore. He liked the children's laughter and when a little face approached him cheery as a fruit loop. On weekends, Ernest left his house through the kitchen door and with his rifle and his forty-five wandered the woods, shooting at any target in sight: a glass bottle, a pinecone, a squirrel. He was as sharp as a Cuisinart. Ernest lived for his lemonade and his guns for many happy years, until suddenly everything started to get blurry and confused. He forgot what day it was and where he was supposed to be, and one day he filled his lemonade stand with his rifle and his forty-five and instead of serving up lemonade, he served up bullets, straight between the eyes.

*(Pause. Lights up on **ELISE** who is in the living room, reading the story from a notebook. **LANEY** turns to her.)*

What do you think?

**ELISE.** It has some nice imagery. I like the little details.

**LANEY.** What details?

**ELISE.** I like the fruit loops. I like the Cuisinart.

**LANEY.** What do you think about the plot?

**ELISE.** The plot is a little gruesome.

**LANEY.** Is it shocking?

**ELISE.** Yes, it's shocking.

**LANEY.** Is it exciting? Did you feel your arm hairs rise like you'd just been electrocuted?

**ELISE.** Electrocuted?

**LANEY.** Yes.

**ELISE.** Maybe not electrocuted.

**LANEY.** Then what?

**ELISE.** The plot could use some work.

**LANEY.** Why?

**ELISE.** Well, the ending comes out of nowhere. Maybe Ernest should take a little longer to deteriorate.

**LANEY.** It's a short story, Mom.

**ELISE.** Yes, Laney. But not all short stories have to be that short.

**LANEY.** I want it to be that short.

**ELISE.** Well then, maybe you should make the ending a little more realistic.

**LANEY.** You always say that.

**ELISE.** I always say what?

**LANEY.** You always want me to be more realistic.

**ELISE.** With your fiction.

**LANEY.** With everything.

**ELISE.** Did you have a bad day at school?

**LANEY.** Did you have a bad day?

**ELISE.** I asked you first.

**LANEY.** So.

**ELISE.** No, I've had a great day.

**LANEY.** Why? What'd you do?

**ELISE.** I made a list. Lists. I listed things.

**LANEY.** Like what?

**ELISE.** Like possible jobs. I made a list of possible jobs in order of preference. You want to hear?

**LANEY.** No.

**ELISE.** Number one: Librarian.
  Number two: Paralegal.
  Number three: Administrative Assistant. NOT not-for-profit.

**LANEY.** What about social work?

**ELISE.** I'm giving up social work.

**LANEY.** Why?

**ELISE.** I'm becoming a misanthrope instead.

**LANEY.** I know what that is.

**ELISE.** I know you know what that is. You're gifted. Too gifted.

**LANEY.** Are we gonna be poor?

**ELISE.** No. Maybe. I should make a list. Ways to avoid being poor:

Number one: get a job.

Number two: marry a rich man.

Number three: marry a rich woman in Vermont or Cleveland, or wherever it is you can marry a rich woman these days.

**LANEY.** You'd have to divorce Dad.

**ELISE.** I have. The papers are filed.

**LANEY.** Oh. Who's going to take care of him?

**ELISE.** The doctors. His parents – your Grandma Liz and Pop – are still there, making sure he's okay. Nothing's changed.

**LANEY.** Except now, he's not your husband. You can get a brand new husband, make me have a brand new Dad.

**ELISE.** Yes, I've made a list. You want to hear it?

**LANEY.** No.

**ELISE.** Number one…

**LANEY.** I'm not playing…

**ELISE.** Holden Caulfield.

(*pause*)

**LANEY.** That's my boyfriend!

**ELISE.** Number Two: Heathcliff.

**LANEY.** Ugh.

**ELISE.** What? He's dark and handsome and mysterious.

**LANEY.** He's whiney.

**ELISE.** No he's not. He's in love.

**LANEY.** Yeah, so in love he ruins the lives of everyone he ever meets.

**ELISE.** You're right. He is kind of a sociopath. Number three: Atticus Finch. Gregory Peck as Atticus Finch.

**LANEY.** He'd be okay.

**ELISE.** Yeah, he would. Neck rub?

**LANEY.** Okay.

(*ELISE massages* **LANEY**'s *neck.*)

**ELISE.** This is good for us.

**LANEY.** What?

**ELISE.** Getting away. Moving back here.

**LANEY.** I never lived here.

**ELISE.** I know, but I did. I never thought I'd move back to this house. But it's not so bad. It's got a lot of character, don't you think?

**LANEY.** It's got mold.

**ELISE.** No it doesn't. Where?

**LANEY.** There. That crack in the wall. It's green.

**ELISE.** That's not mold. That's moss. I think.

**LANEY.** Same thing.

**ELISE.** Well I'm glad we're here. This is going to be a good change for us.

**LANEY.** It's good for my writing.

**ELISE.** How so?

**LANEY.** Suffering is good for writing.

**ELISE.** Suffering is not good for writing. Suffering is good for depression. Reading is good for writing. Reading William Faulkner. He lived here, you know.

**LANEY.** I know. You've said that like a zillon times.

**ELISE.** I keep thinking you're going to be impressed.

**LANEY.** I am. He's on my Best American Authors list twice.

**ELISE.** How can he be on it twice?

**LANEY.** Two of his books are on it.

**ELISE.** Which two?

**LANEY.** *The Sound and the Fury* and *As I Lay Dying.*

**ELISE.** Did you make up that list?

**LANEY.** No. Mr. Caruthers wrote it.

**ELISE.** Oh God.

**LANEY.** What?

**ELISE.** Mr. Caruthers was a failed writer trapped in a middle school library.

**LANEY.** I liked him. You should like him. You both make lists.

**ELISE.** He's a fish. A carp.

**LANEY.** A carp?

**ELISE.** Yes. A scaly, slippery carp.

**LANEY.** I think he had bedroom eyes.

**ELISE.** What do you know about bedroom eyes? You better not know anything about bedroom eyes.

**LANEY.** Bedroom eyes are eyes that make you want to go to bed.

**ELISE.** Who would want to go to bed with a carp?

**LANEY.** Me!

**ELISE.** Elizabeth Lane Waters…

**LANEY.** Mom! I'm kidding. Geesh…I wouldn't go to bed with Mr. Caruthers. He's like forty.

**ELISE.** You better not go to bed with anyone.

**LANEY.** Mom, who would want to go to bed with me?

**ELISE.** Laney…baby…

(ELISE *pulls* LANEY *towards her.* LANEY *pulls away.*)

I'm not finished.

**LANEY.** That's enough.

**ELISE.** You said it helps.

**LANEY.** It doesn't help. The doctors said.

**ELISE.** It makes you feel better.

**LANEY.** But it doesn't help. Not really.

(*pause*)

**ELISE.** He hit on me once.

**LANEY.** Who?

**ELISE.** The carp. At a P.T.A. meeting. When Peter first got sick.

**LANEY.** Gross.

**ELISE.** I thought you said he had bedroom eyes.

**LANEY.** A carp can't have bedroom eyes.

**ELISE.** No, you're right. A carp can't have bedroom eyes. You look tired, Laney.

**LANEY.** I'm not tired.

**ELISE.** Yes, you are. You have bedroom eyes. Eyes that want to go to bed.

**LANEY.** I have work to do.

**ELISE.** Homework?

**LANEY.** No, my work.

**ELISE.** You're fourteen. You don't have work that's not homework. Child labor laws.

**LANEY.** I have my writing.

**ELISE.** You've written enough for today.

**LANEY.** I have to fix the plot. You're the one who said I have to fix the ending, and so I have to stay up and fix it. It's your fault!

**ELISE.** You don't have to fix it tonight.

**LANEY.** Yes I do. You shouldn't be so picky if you want me to go to bed on time.

**ELISE.** It's time for bed.

**LANEY.** Why can't you just leave me alone?

**ELISE.** Oh, let me see...yes, that's right, I'm your mother.

**LANEY.** God, I hate you!

**ELISE.** Oh, go to hell, Laney. *(pause)* I'm sorry. I'm so sorry. I shouldn't have said that. It's a hard time for us. For me. Forgive me?

**LANEY.** No.

**ELISE.** Forgive me tomorrow?

**LANEY.** Maybe. It has to be perfect. I'm going to show it to somebody.

**ELISE.** Who?

**LANEY.** A girl at school. She likes my writing.

**ELISE.** You made a friend?

**LANEY.** Don't look so surprised.

## Scene Two

*(Earlier the same day. Outside the high school.* **MARI-
BEL** *sits on the stadium bleachers, finishing her lunch.*
**LANEY** *approaches her.)*

**LANEY.** Hi.

**MARIBEL.** Hello.

**LANEY.** I didn't know we could eat out here.

**MARIBEL.** We're not supposed to.

**LANEY.** Oh.

**MARIBEL.** I just hate it in there.

**LANEY.** Me too.

**MARIBEL.** You could eat here.

**LANEY.** Okay.

**MARIBEL.** The security guard comes out here sometimes. I
just hide beneath the bleachers when I see him.

**LANEY.** You're a rebel.

**MARIBEL.** No. I'm just Maribel.

**LANEY.** Laney.

**MARIBEL.** You're new, aren't you?

**LANEY.** Yeah.

**MARIBEL.** Where'd you move from?

**LANEY.** Madison, Wisconsin. But my Mom grew up here.

**MARIBEL.** I was new last year.

**LANEY.** Yeah? Where from?

**MARIBEL.** Nowhere. I mean, I didn't move. I used to be
home schooled by my Mom, but she got in trouble
because she never got registered as a home school
teacher or something, so now I go here.

**LANEY.** Oh.

**MARIBEL.** But I'm behind. I have to take some of my classes
with freshmen. It's so embarrassing.

**LANEY.** You don't have any classes with me.

**MARIBEL.** You're probably in advanced classes. You look
advanced.

LANEY. I'm not. I'm not advanced.

MARIBEL. You look advanced.

LANEY. I'm not.

MARIBEL. I wish I were advanced. But I'm remedial. Remedial is worse than being advanced. Remedial is like being retarded.

LANEY. No, it's not. It just means you need to catch up is all.

MARIBEL. You're nice.

LANEY. Thanks.

(pause)

MARIBEL. So, have you found a church yet?

LANEY. Church?

MARIBEL. Yeah.

LANEY. No. I don't go to church.

MARIBEL. So, you don't know about Jesus then?

LANEY. What about him?

MARIBEL. That he died for you. That he died for you to save you from sin?

LANEY. Oh, I don't believe in sin.

MARIBEL. Why not?

LANEY. I just don't.

MARIBEL. You're kinda funny looking with your back and all.

LANEY. Thanks.

MARIBEL. Anyone talk to you since you came to this school?

LANEY. The teachers. You.

MARIBEL. Any other students?

LANEY. No.

MARIBEL. See. That's sin.

LANEY. Whatever.

MARIBEL. Don't feel bad.

LANEY. I don't.

**MARIBEL.** I get sinned against all the time in this school – Deedee Cummings pulled down my pants in gym class today – but I don't mind, because I know that the things of this earth, they're not lasting. *(pause)* You think I'm a freak, don't you?

**LANEY.** No.

**MARIBEL.** Yes, you do. I can tell.

**LANEY.** Well, yeah. You're kinda freaky.

**MARIBEL.** I know it's kinda freaky to bring up Jesus when I've only just met you, but look at it this way: I mean, you could die tomorrow, you could die this afternoon – you know a car wreck, or a heart attack or something – and at least, I would know that you didn't die not ever having heard of Jesus, and maybe, just maybe, because of this conversation, because I talked to you about Jesus, when those headlights are facing the passenger seat and you know you're about to meet your end, you'll remember Jesus and how much he loves you and you'll ask him into your heart right then and there before you die, and then you won't have to face everlasting hell.

**LANEY.** I don't believe in everlasting hell.

**MARIBEL.** But there has to be punishment for people who sin and sin and keep sinning. If there isn't everlasting hell, then Hitler and Stalin and Deedee Cummings will never get punished for what they did. All the people in this school who ignore you will never get punished either.

**LANEY.** That's one way of looking at it, I guess.

**MARIBEL.** Thank you. I think you're very pretty anyway. I mean, even with the hump and all.

**LANEY.** It's not a hump.

**MARIBEL.** What is it then?

**LANEY.** It's the muscles in my back. They're working against one another. It's called dystonia. Having a humpback is called kyphosis. I don't have kyphosis. I have dystonia. It's different. It's temporary. I'm glad I have it.

**MARIBEL.** You are?

**LANEY.** Yeah. I'm glad I have it, because it has shown me how shallow people are here. At my old school in Wisconsin, where I used to go before my dystonia got bad, I had lots of friends, in lots of different groups. I was going to be on the Homecoming court. I mean, they hadn't had elections, but everyone told me I was going to be on it. Not that I really wanted to be on it. Homecoming court's kinda lame and all, but I would've been on it. Here, nobody talks to me. But I haven't changed. My essential personality hasn't changed. So I know the reason they don't talk to me is because of my dystonia, and I'm glad I have it, because now I know how shallow people are. It's a good thing to know, don't you think?

**MARIBEL.** Yes, it is. You would have looked amazing on Homecoming Court, especially if you put your hair in a French twist. I could do it for you.

**LANEY.** Maybe later.

**MARIBEL.** I didn't mean now. I meant for when you get elected to the Homecoming Court. Next year when your back gets better and everyone realizes how pretty you are, and I'll lose all my baby fat and grow new skin. We'll be on the Homecoming Court together!

**LANEY.** Except we'll turn it down, because the Homecoming court is lame.

**MARIBEL.** Completely!

(*They laugh, a little tentatively still.* **LANEY** *grimaces.*)

**MARIBEL.** Does it hurt?

**LANEY.** Sometimes.

**MARIBEL.** Can I touch it?

**LANEY.** No!

**MARIBEL.** It's just…when someone's sick at church, we pray for them. We lay hands on them. It helps sometimes. Sometimes Jesus chooses to make them feel better. Sometimes he doesn't though.

**LANEY.** Why is that?

**MARIBEL.** I don't know. It's one of God's mysteries. Like my little brother, Gabriel. He was born with a cleft lip. No one knows why. It's one of God's mysteries. People used to gasp when they saw him. Does that happen to you?

**LANEY.** No.

**MARIBEL.** When Deedee Cummings pulled down my pants, the whole room gasped. Like they all took in one big gulp of air together. And then they laughed. Afterwards Melissa Jenkins put her arm around me, real nice like, like she was gonna take care of me, but when we got to the locker room, she handed me a razor, and said I should use it to shave my pubes so I'd look better the next time.

**LANEY.** I meant to say, yes. I've had that happen. Not the pubes thing. But the gasping.

**MARIBEL.** Do you want to come to church with me on Friday?

**LANEY.** I don't know. What's it like?

**MARIBEL.** Well, there's a band. Piano, drums. Marcus Grayson used to the play the guitar, but he doesn't come anymore.

**LANEY.** I know who he is. He's a Junior. He has bedroom eyes.

**MARIBEL.** Yes, he does. But he doesn't come anymore, so now there's only the piano and the drums. My Dad's the preacher.

**LANEY.** He is?

**MARIBEL.** Yeah, but he also sells cars, used cars like Hondas and Mitsubishis, because the church is small and can't afford to pay his whole salary. I was going to get a Mitsubishi for my sixteenth birthday, but then I couldn't because I failed the test. When the tape said to turn on the right blinker, I turned on the left. That's a stupid reason to fail a test, I know, I just got so nervous. What does your Dad do?

**LANEY.** I don't have a Dad.

**MARIBEL.** Is he dead?

**LANEY.** Yeah.

**MARIBEL.** Do you miss him?

**LANEY.** I don't want to talk about it, okay?

**MARIBEL.** Sure. But going to church, you know, it might help.

**LANEY.** Okay. I'll go.

**MARIBEL.** Really?

**LANEY.** Sure.

(**MARIBEL** *hugs* **LANEY.**)

It's no big deal.

**MARIBEL.** No one in this entire school has ever agreed to go to church with me!

**LANEY.** Well, new experiences are good for my writing. That's why I said yes. Not because I need help.

**MARIBEL.** You're a writer?

**LANEY.** Yes.

**MARIBEL.** I've never met a writer.

**LANEY.** You want to read one of my stories? I wrote it during second period.

**MARIBEL.** Okay.

(**LANEY** *takes a notebook out of her backpack.*)

**LANEY.** It's a first draft, so it's not perfect or anything. You're the first person I've shown it to.

**MARIBEL.** Really?

**LANEY.** Yeah.

(**LANEY** *hands the open notebook to* **MARIBEL** *who reads the story silently. She looks up at* **LANEY,** *eyes shining.*)

**MARIBEL.** Wow. That's intense. You're the most talented person I've ever met.

(**LANEY** *grins.*)

**LANEY.** Thanks.

**MARIBEL.** Can I tell you a secret?

**LANEY.** Yeah.

**MARIBEL.** You swear you won't tell anyone? Promise to God?

**LANEY.** Yeah, I promise.

**MARIBEL.** I think I have stigmata.

**LANEY.** You mean, like when you bleed from your hands and feet?

**MARIBEL.** No, not that kind. I read about stigmata on the internet in the library, and I think I have the invisible kind, where you feel the pain in your hands but there's no blood.

**LANEY.** What pain?

**MARIBEL.** The pain of Jesus. The pain of the whole world.

**LANEY.** In your hands?

**MARIBEL.** Yeah.

**LANEY.** That's intense.

**MARIBEL.** It is.

**LANEY.** What does it feel like?

**MARIBEL.** It feels like my veins are about to pop, and they…

(**MARIBEL** *looks down at the notebook.*)

They "bulge beneath my skin like big blue worms, squirming just below the dirt."

(**LANEY** *squeals in delight; she can't help herself.*)

What?

**LANEY.** No one's ever quoted me before!

## Scene Three

*(MARIBEL and LANEY sit in the living room.)*

**MARIBEL.** I wish you could spend the night Friday.

**LANEY.** Why'd she say no?

**MARIBEL.** Because she's a you-know-what.

**LANEY.** No, what?

**MARIBEL.** You know.

**LANEY.** No, I don't. What?

**MARIBEL.** You know what.

**LANEY.** No, I don't know what. What?

**MARIBEL.** Stop it!

*(The girls burst into laughter. ELISE enters with a bag of groceries, a carton of cigarettes poking up out of the bag.)*

**ELISE.** You must be Maribel.

**MARIBEL.** Yes. Do you smoke?

**ELISE.** Yes.

**MARIBEL.** You shouldn't smoke.

**ELISE.** You shouldn't judge.

**LANEY.** Mom!

**ELISE.** Right. Sorry. I've taken up bad habits in my spare time. Biting my nails, tweezing the hairs on my legs one at a time, smoking. But you shouldn't smoke, or bite your nails, or tweeze the hairs on your legs one at a time. It may not give you lung cancer, but it definitely makes your legs red and blotchy, you know, like when you get razor burn down there…

**LANEY.** Mom!

**ELISE.** What? Am I an embarrassment?

**LANEY.** Mom's unemployed.

**ELISE.** It's making me a little nuts. Sorry.

**MARIBEL.** I forgive you.

**ELISE.** Thanks. What are you two up to?

**LANEY.** None of your business.

**ELISE.** Well, would you like a cocktail to go with that? Coke, sprite, milk?

**MARIBEL & LANEY.** Sprite.

*(They burst out laughing.)*

**LANEY.** We're synchronized.

**MARIBEL.** On the same brain plane.

**ELISE.** I see.

*(ELISE starts to exit for the kitchen.)*

**MARIBEL.** Mrs. Waters…

**ELISE.** Elise. Call me Elise.

**MARIBEL.** Elise, have you ever asked Jesus into your heart?

**ELISE.** No.

**MARIBEL.** Do you want to?

**ELISE.** No.

*(ELISE exits.)*

**LANEY.** You shouldn't bring that Jesus stuff up around my Mom.

**MARIBEL.** I knew it wasn't the right moment, but I just thought, what if she had a heart attack or a stray bullet hit her while she was in the kitchen, and she died, and I never told her about Jesus, and then that would always be with me you know, that I had this opportunity and didn't use it.

**LANEY.** A stray bullet?

**MARIBEL.** I know. It's not likely, but there was a drive by shooting here once.

**LANEY.** What do you mean here?

**MARIBEL.** Well, not right here. But nearby the college.

*(ELISE returns, gives a can of Sprite to the girls.)*

**ELISE.** There you go.

**LANEY.** Maribel and me, we're going to the school dance on Friday. Okay?

**ELISE.** Really?

**LANEY.** Yes.

**ELISE.** I thought you said you hated school dances, that they were humiliating drills in gender oppression.

**LANEY.** You said that. In Madison. I said the gym stinks too bad to want to dance in it.

**ELISE.** Right. Why the change of mind?

**LANEY.** Maribel wants to go, don't you Maribel?

**MARIBEL.** Uh huh. I want to dance with boys.

**ELISE.** How old are you, Maribel?

**MARIBEL.** Sixteen.

**ELISE.** And you two have classes together?

**MARIBEL.** Oh no. Laney's too advanced to have classes with me.

**LANEY.** Maribel was home schooled, but her Mom never got certified, so she's behind. She's really smart about literature though. She's a great critic. The best.

**ELISE.** Oh. *(to MARIBEL.)* What books do you like?

**MARIBEL.** I like short stories.

**ELISE.** What short stories?

**MARIBEL.** Laney's.

**ELISE.** I see. So what do your parents do, Maribel?

**MARIBEL.** My Dad's a preacher. Of the Church of the Redeemer. It's a holiness church, but we don't pick up snakes or drink poison, or any of that crazy stuff. Just full submersion baptism, prophecy, healing, and speaking in tongues.

**ELISE.** Do you speak in tongues?

**MARIBEL.** No, I don't have that gift. Laney, we should pray and see if you have it though. Maybe you have the gift of tongues, and I could interpret, since we're on the same brain plane.

**ELISE.** Interpret?

**MARIBEL.** Yeah. When someone in the church speaks in tongues, sometimes another person interprets. Like when God has a message he wants someone in the church to hear. My Mom and Dad were given a prophesy of my brother Gabriel having a cleft lip. God gave the message to Mom in tongues, and then sister Rebecca interpreted. She said, "be comforted in your deformity." And then Gabriel was born with a cleft lip.

**ELISE.** Seems kind of vague. We all have deformities. Emotional ones at least.

**LANEY.** Mom, I don't think God meant it as a metaphor.

**ELISE.** How do you know what God meant?

**LANEY.** How do you know? You don't even believe in God.

**ELISE.** Neither do you, young lady!

**LANEY.** Maybe I do.

**ELISE.** Oh really?

**LANEY.** Well, I believe in sin, I believe in that much.

**ELISE.** You believe in sin?

**LANEY.** Yes. Hurting people, ignoring people, *divorcing people*. That's sin.

**ELISE.** Watch it, Laney.

**MARIBEL.** Sin is what keeps us from God.

**ELISE.** No, rationality is what keeps us from God. Seeing the world as it really is keeps us from buying into a patriarchal mythology that has kept women oppressed for centuries.

**LANEY.** Mom!

**ELISE.** What? Aren't I allowed to express my opinions?

**LANEY.** No!

**MARIBEL.** What do you mean?

**LANEY.** What?

**MARIBEL.** *(to* **ELISE***)* What you just said.

**ELISE.** It means, honey, that religion has been used to keep women from pursuing their full potential.

**MARIBEL.** I don't feel that way.

**ELISE.** Well, you don't right now. But trust me, you don't want to find yourself having to obey some backwards Bible thumper who will only let you out of the house to go to church and to pick up a box of diapers at the Piggily Wiggily.

**MARIBEL.** I don't plan on getting married.

**ELISE.** Well, then the only choice you have is to live a life of celibacy, which trust me, is no fun. People need to have sex.

**LANEY.** Mom!

**ELISE.** What? I just think Maribel should seriously consider her options before she makes up her mind completely.

**LANEY.** She didn't ask for your opinion.

**ELISE.** Do you want my opinion, Maribel?

**MARIBEL.** Yes.

**ELISE.** See? Laney never wants my opinion about anything. She thinks I'm too critical.

**LANEY.** Maribel just said that to be nice, didn't you Maribel?

**ELISE.** Did you? Were you just being nice?

**MARIBEL.** I don't know.

**ELISE.** It's okay, honey. Just don't believe everything your Daddy says in the pulpit. And don't believe everything Laney says either, for that matter.

**LANEY.** Get out of here!

**ELISE.** I'm going. You two have fun. But I'm keeping my ear to the door. Absolutely no speaking in tongues.

**LANEY.** Get out!!!

**ELISE.** I mean it.

(**ELISE** *exits.*)

**MARIBEL.** I don't want to get married, because I plan on giving my life to God entirely. But I wish I could have sex. I'm still a virgin. I've been fingered once, but you can be fingered and still be a virgin.

**LANEY.** Maribel…just shut up for a minute okay!

**MARIBEL.** Why? What'd I say?

**LANEY.** It's just…maybe you shouldn't talk so much. You sound stupid sometimes.

**MARIBEL.** I'm not. I'm not stupid.

**LANEY.** I know you're not. But sometimes that's how you sound.

(**MARIBEL,** *clearly distressed, starts rubbing her palm.*)

**LANEY.** *(continued)* What's wrong? Are you like going to cry?

**MARIBEL.** No, no I'm not. *(pause)* I'm gonna go wait outside for my Mom. She'll be here soon.

**LANEY.** You want me to wait with you?

**MARIBEL.** No.

**LANEY.** Okay. I'll call you tonight.

**MARIBEL.** If you want.

**LANEY.** I do. I do want to.

**MARIBEL.** Okay. Bye.

**LANEY.** Bye.

## Scene Four

*(LANEY reads the following story to the audience. ELISE sits in the living room behind her. She cannot hear LANEY.)*

LANEY. Veronica's young life was marked by one constant thing: the cruelty of her Mother...Eliza, who having stolen Veronica from her Father when she was a baby, now forced her to clean every floor in the house until it shone like aluminum foil. The only escape Veronica had from Eliza was when she rode her bike as far away from the house as she could, the cool September air filling her lungs full to capacity, just like she had filled the tires on her bike full to capacity with her bike pump. One day, Eliza found the kitchen floors not to her liking, and so she confiscated Veronica's bike and gave it to the Salvation Army (Eliza liked to keep up the pretense of being a good person to the outside world). This was the last straw for Veronica, who decided she could stand it no more. So in the middle of the night, she snuck into Eliza's room, stuck her bike pump into Eliza's belly button and filled her so full of air, she exploded, her bits and pieces decorating the walls.

The End.

*(LANEY turns to ELISE and stares at her triumphantly. ELISE looks up at LANEY questioningly, wearily.)*

## Scene Five

*(LANEY and MARIBEL sit in the church choir loft. It is
dark. MARIBEL hands a flashlight to LANEY. They turn
on the flashlights.)*

**LANEY.** I like the sanctuary like this. Empty.

**MARIBEL.** You said you liked the service.

**LANEY.** I did. I just like it better like this. Quiet.

**MARIBEL.** You said you wanted to convert. If you convert,
you have to go to service.

**LANEY.** I know.

**MARIBEL.** You could have converted during the service.

**LANEY.** I didn't want to convert during the service. I want
to convert with you. Alone. There's nothing wrong
with that, is there?

**MARIBEL.** No.

**LANEY.** I like your Mom.

**MARIBEL.** Why?

**LANEY.** She's quiet. My Mom's never quiet. I'm still not talking to her. She's so embarrassing, God…

**MARIBEL.** You can't do that.

**LANEY.** What?

**MARIBEL.** Take the Lord's name in vain like that. If you're
going to convert, you have to stop doing that.

**LANEY.** Okay.

**MARIBEL.** Are you ready?

**LANEY.** We should eat first. I brought some cake from the
potluck.

**MARIBEL.** We can't eat in here.

**LANEY.** Come on. It's a special occasion. I'm gonna get
saved, right?

**MARIBEL.** Yes.

*(LANEY hands MARIBEL a piece of cake. They eat.)*

I told my parents we were playing flashlight tag with
the youth group. The youth group always plays flashlight tag on Friday nights.

**LANEY.** Why couldn't you just say we'd be here?

**MARIBEL.** We're not supposed to be here.

**LANEY.** Why not? I'm converting, right? They want me to convert, don't they?

**MARIBEL.** Well you're not supposed to sneak into the sanctuary to convert. You're supposed to convert during the service, walk to the front of the church while everybody sings, "Just as I am."

**LANEY.** I like this way better.

**MARIBEL.** Me too. *(pause)* The adults, they all think flashlight tag is a Godly kind of fun. But it's not. I got fingered playing flashlight tag.

**LANEY.** How'd that happen?

**MARIBEL.** The whole point of playing flashlight tag is so you can hang out in the dark woods with boys. One night, I was wearing a skirt, and Marcus Grayson told me to come hide with him in this dry creek bed, and while we were crouching there, I felt his fingers all of a sudden walking up my leg. I didn't move. But they kept walking up my thigh, until he fingered me.

**LANEY.** Did it hurt?

**MARIBEL.** No, it didn't hurt. It felt good. Kinda. I just wish he had kissed me is all. I've never been kissed. Have you?

**LANEY.** Sure. I kissed a boy at my school in Wisconsin. Quentin Compson. We kissed in the library after school. We frenched. And then we got interrupted by Mr. Caruthers.

**MARIBEL.** Who's that?

**LANEY.** The librarian. He was cool though. We didn't get in trouble or anything. Mr. Caruthers just sent us outside.

**MARIBEL.** Have you ever been fingered?

**LANEY.** No.

**MARIBEL.** Well, if you want to get fingered, we can go play flashlight tag. Marcus Grayson isn't here, but Henry Bowen is, and he tries to finger everyone. He'd try to finger you, even though you got, you know, a hump.

**LANEY.** It's not a hump. I think it's slutty to be fingered.

**MARIBEL.** It's not like having sex. You can be fingered and still be a virgin.

**LANEY.** It's still slutty. Especially if the person doesn't kiss you.

**MARIBEL.** The next time I tried to hide with Marcus I followed him through the woods, but he kept zigzagging back and forth through the trees. When I finally caught up with him and tried to hold his hand, he said, "get away from me, you big fat cow." I laid down on the ground in the woods and got stigmata.

**LANEY.** I don't really think you're slutty. Marcus Grayson is an asswad.

**MARIBEL.** *(giggling)* You can't say that here.

**LANEY.** What?

**MARIBEL.** You can't cuss.

**LANEY.** I didn't cuss. I just said asswad.

**MARIBEL.** You said it again.

**LANEY.** You mean asswad?

**MARIBEL.** *(laughing even harder)* Laney, I'm serious.

**LANEY.** Don't be such a tightass.

**MARIBEL.** Laney!

**LANEY.** Asswad, tight ass, asshole, asinine.

**MARIBEL.** Stop it!

**LANEY.** Asinine is not a cuss word.

**MARIBEL.** It's not funny.

**LANEY.** Then why are you laughing?

**MARIBEL.** Because you're not being serious.

**LANEY.** I'm as serious as a cereal box.

*(The laughing subsides. They both calm down a little.)*

**MARIBEL.** Are you ready now?

**LANEY.** I guess.

**MARIBEL.** You have to be sure. It doesn't count if you're not sure.

**LANEY.** I'm sure. What do I have to do?

**MARIBEL.** First you have to confess your sin.

**LANEY.** Okay. I confess my sin.

**MARIBEL.** No, you have to be specific. List all your sins.

**LANEY.** Aloud?

**MARIBEL.** Yeah. It's the first step in getting saved.

**LANEY.** Give me an example.

**MARIBEL.** Okay. Dear Jesus, please forgive me for allowing Marcus Grayson to finger me. Cause even though being fingered isn't as bad as having sex, it's still a sin.

**LANEY.** But I've never been fingered.

**MARIBEL.** Well, you just have to list your other sins.

**LANEY.** Okay. Like what?

**MARIBEL.** Like drunkenness and sloth and greed. Holding other idols before God. Stealing. Murder. Cussing.

**LANEY.** Dear Jesus, please forgive me for saying ass.

*(They both start giggling.)*

**MARIBEL.** You're not supposed to laugh.

**LANEY.** I'm sorry. It's just funny. The word, ass.

**MARIBEL.** Do you want Jesus to come into your heart or not?

**LANEY.** I guess. What's it feel like? When Jesus comes into your heart?

**MARIBEL.** It feels…it feels like even if nobody ever speaks to you, or hears you, or even touches you ever again, it doesn't matter, because everything's okay. All the pain you feel, it just goes away and everything's okay. Someone sees me and hears me and knows everywhere that I hurt. And he just takes all that pain on himself, so I don't have to feel it anymore. So I'm whole. So I'm healed.

**LANEY.** I'd like that. To be healed.

**MARIBEL.** You want me to help you confess?

**LANEY.** Okay.

**MARIBEL.** Close your eyes and repeat after me. Dear Jesus…

**LANEY.** Dear Jesus…

**MARIBEL.** Please forgive me for my sins.

**LANEY.** Please forgive me for my sins.

**MARIBEL.** For using your name in vain…

**LANEY.** For using your name in vain…

**MARIBEL.** And for ignoring you for fourteen years…

**LANEY.** And for ignoring you for fourteen years…

**MARIBEL.** For my lustful thoughts and hurtful deeds…

**LANEY.** For my lustful thoughts and hurtful deeds…

**MARIBEL.** I ask forgiveness.

**LANEY.** I ask forgiveness.

**MARIBEL.** You say that if we confess with our mouths that you are God and if we believe in our hearts that you were raised from the dead, then we will be saved. Elizabeth Lane Waters, do you confess?

**LANEY.** I confess.

**MARIBEL.** Do you believe?

**LANEY.** I believe.

**MARIBEL.** Now ask Jesus to come into your heart.

**LANEY.** Come into my heart Jesus!

    *(pause)*

**MARIBEL.** What do you feel?

    *(pause)*

**LANEY.** Nothing. I feel nothing. It didn't work.

**MARIBEL.** You have to mean it.

**LANEY.** I meant it!

**MARIBEL.** You have to really mean it.

**LANEY.** I really meant it.

**MARIBEL.** If you really meant it, it would work.

**LANEY.** It didn't. I really meant it, and it didn't work.

**MARIBEL.** That's not possible. Let's do it again.

**LANEY.** I'm not doing it again. I asked Jesus into my heart, and he didn't enter.

**MARIBEL.** Jesus doesn't say no!

**LANEY.** He did to me.

**MARIBEL.** Laney, we have to try again.

**LANEY.** I'm not trying again. You can't make me try again.

**MARIBEL.** But I don't want you to go to hell.

**LANEY.** I don't believe in hell.

**MARIBEL.** I don't want you to go to hell, because you're the only friend I've ever had.

**LANEY.** You don't need friends. You have Jesus.

MARIBEL. I need you. I love you, Laney.

LANEY. You do?

MARIBEL. Yes. Let me pray for you. If you won't try again, let me pray for you, okay?

(*LANEY nods.*)

(**MARIBEL** *grabs* **LANEY**'s *hand, closes her eyes and prays for her fervently.*)

MARIBEL. *(con't.)* Dear Jesus, it's Maribel. Maribel and my friend Laney. I ask that you forgive me of my sins, for thinking so much about Marcus Grayson and being fingered. I pray that you forgive me for wanting to kill Melissa Jenkins and Deedee Cummings. I pray that you'll help me to forgive them. Forgive me for the hatred in my heart. But most of all, I ask that you forgive me for not being a better witness to Laney, because if I had been a better witness, I know that she would have felt you, because I know you never say no to anybody, and if Laney thought you said no, it must be because I did something wrong. I pray that you enter Laney's heart, dear Jesus, so that she won't have to suffer everlasting hell, because Lord, she is so beautiful and full of gifts, like her writing, and I know that you'll want to keep her near you always. Lord, I know you have mysterious ways and that I can't know your every hair, the way you know my every hair, but I know that you don't say no, so Lord, I'm asking that you forgive me, forgive me, not for myself, but so Laney might be healed by you too. Amen.

(**MARIBEL** *opens her eyes, glistening. She looks at* **LANEY**. *Silence. It's electric. Slowly,* **MARIBEL** *smiles.*)

MARIBEL. Do you feel that?

LANEY. Yes.

MARIBEL. Do you know what it is?

(*LANEY shakes her head.*)

It's the holy ghost.

(**LANEY** *leans in and kisses* **MARIBEL** *on the mouth. It is sweet and gentle and a beat too long.*)

## Scene Six

*(The living room. ELISE is up, waiting for LANEY. She has a glass of wine, and the bottle sits beside the chair. When she hears LANEY enter, she hides the bottle.)*

**ELISE.** How was it?

**LANEY.** Fine.

**ELISE.** Did you dance?

**LANEY.** Some.

**ELISE.** Really? Who with?

**LANEY.** Maribel.

**ELISE.** Did you take your medicine?

**LANEY.** God…I'm not a baby.

**ELISE.** I know. You want some hot chocolate? I could make some hot chocolate. Not the crap packaged kind. The from scratch kind. With marshmallows. And a peppermint stick.

**LANEY.** I'm not hungry.

**ELISE.** Sit down.

**LANEY.** I'm not talking to you.

**ELISE.** I've noticed. But you can sit down, can't you? Sit with me and not talk. We can sit in silence. With chocolate and marshmallows and peppermint goodness and your favorite movie of all time: *The Bicycle Thief.*

**LANEY.** That's not my favorite movie of all time. That's your favorite movie of all time.

**ELISE.** That's right. You prefer *The Goonies.*

**LANEY.** I do not.

**ELISE.** You love *The Goonies.*

**LANEY.** Do not.

**ELISE.** You used to love *The Goonies.* What do you love now? What does my beautiful grown-up girl love now?

**LANEY.** Being left alone.

**ELISE.** I don't believe you.

**LANEY.** Why did you have to attack Maribel like that?

**ELISE.** I didn't attack her.

**LANEY.** You did so. You insulted her religion.

**ELISE.** I expressed an opinion. I'm sorry if it embarrassed you. *(pause)* Do you want to talk about your Dad?

**LANEY.** No! God…

**ELISE.** I think you're upset about your Dad. I think that's why things have been rough between us. I think Gregory Peck is turning out to be a sorry step-father.

**LANEY.** I hate it when you do that!

**ELISE.** What?

**LANEY.** Make jokes like that. It's not funny.

**ELISE.** I joke, therefore, I cope.

**LANEY.** God…

**ELISE.** Laney, you're so old. How did you get to be so old?

**LANEY.** Have you been drinking? Are you drunk?

**ELISE.** Not drunk. Buzzed. I'm not a drunkard. I'm a buzzard.

**LANEY.** I'm going to my room.

**ELISE.** I got a job. That's why I'm having a glass, a bottle, of wine. To celebrate.

**LANEY.** You got a job?

**ELISE.** I did. I'm a busy, buzzard of a bee. I got a job.

**LANEY.** That's great, Mom. You need a job. You're crazy without a job, you know.

**ELISE.** You're looking at the new office manager, that's right, office manager, not administrative assistant, for Jerry L. Startler, Esq. He's a torts lawyer. Ambulance chaser. He wore a seersucker suit. My Father wore a seersucker suit. I think that's why I said yes. It's a horrible job.

**LANEY.** You don't know. You haven't started yet. Maybe he'll let you make lists.

**ELISE.** Right. Ways to find clients: One, bribe ambulance drivers. Two, stake out the chiropractor's office. Three, go under cover as an E.M.T.

**LANEY.** You could go back to social work.

**ELISE.** No more social work. This is the beginning of my new life. No more social work. Jerry L. Startler Esq. pays better than social work. And he seemed grateful that I took the job, even though he's a Torts lawyer. That's the secret ill of social work, Laney. The people you try to help, they aren't grateful. They're suspicious and mostly crazy. Poor people are not saints. They're just poor and stupid and often crazy. Rich people are often stupid and crazy too, but they're rich. So all things being equal, I'll take the rich and stupid over the poor and stupid, because the rich, they can pay, and I'm in a place in life where I want to get paid.

**LANEY.** That's great, Mom.

**ELISE.** But after I said yes, and Jerry L. Startler, Esq. shook my hand, oozing gratitude, I got into my car and cried. I just sat there and cried, cause now I'm the kind of person who wants to get paid. Isn't life grand?

**LANEY.** I guess.

**ELISE.** Laney, stay and sit with me, cuddle with me. I can't take your petulant teenage thing tonight. Stay and be my little girl. I need my little girl, my Flopsy. I have nobody else in the whole wide world. Stay.

(**LANEY** *sits next to* **ELISE. ELISE** *cuddles her.*)

Are you my Flopsy?

**LANEY.** Yes.

**ELISE.** And who am I?

**LANEY.** Mom…

**ELISE.** I'm your Mopsy. *(Pause)* Who do you love?

**LANEY.** You know.

**ELISE.** Tell me. Tell me who you love.

**LANEY.** I love you, Mom.

**ELISE.** That's right. My little girl loves me, and I don't need anything else? Do I? Do I?

**LANEY.** No.

(**ELISE** *sits up and starts to massage* **LANEY**'s *neck.*)

**ELISE.** And I'm going to start being less embarrassing. I am. Starting now, I am going to be the most un-embarrassing Mom ever. Your friends will always be welcome here, even the crazy religious kind. I'll bite my tongue, when they evangelize, I promise. I'll chalk it up to the hazard of moving South again. Even though I hate it. I'll bite my tongue, okay?

**LANEY.** Okay. *(pause)* If I tell you something, will you promise not to get mad?

**ELISE.** What is it?

**LANEY.** Promise you won't get mad.

**ELISE.** Promise I won't get mad.

**LANEY.** It's two things really.

**ELISE.** You can tell me anything.

**LANEY.** I'm a lesbian.

*(ELISE stops massaging LANEY's neck.)*

**ELISE.** Really? Since when?

**LANEY.** Since tonight. And I've been saved. I'm a holiness lesbian.

**ELISE.** A holiness lesbian?

**LANEY.** Yes. I believe in the power of the holy ghost, and I kiss girls. And I didn't go to the dance, so I guess that makes three things you can't get mad about.

**ELISE.** You didn't go to the dance?

**LANEY.** No. I went to church with Maribel. And then I got saved. And then we kissed.

**ELISE.** You kissed Maribel?

**LANEY.** On the mouth.

**ELISE.** Laney…

**LANEY.** You promised you wouldn't get mad.

**ELISE.** I'm not mad. I'm sober. Suddenly, I'm sober.

**LANEY.** And I'm glad that I'm a holiness lesbian. I'm proud. If there were a holiness lesbian march, I'd march. It's a good thing.

**ELISE.** I didn't say it wasn't.

**LANEY.** But you wouldn't march, would you? You wouldn't march to support my lifestyle.

**ELISE.** Lifestyle? You have a lifestyle now? Where do you hear these things?

**LANEY.** I don't hear them anywhere. It's who I am.

**ELISE.** Laney, one evening is not a lifestyle.

**LANEY.** Don't try to make this not a big deal. It's a very big deal.

**ELISE.** Yes, it is a big deal, Laney. And I'm just trying to deal with it, so don't put on the dramatics. Come back to earth for a little while. I'm not oppressing you, I'm just taking it all in.

**LANEY.** Are you going to disown me?

**ELISE.** Laney, of course not. Be realistic.

**LANEY.** Don't say that! I hate it when you say that!

**ELISE.** Calm down. Look, if you're a lesbian, I'm fine with that. And if you want to join the holiness church of the redeemer, then I'm fine with that too, although admittedly less so. But I also think you're a little confused, because the pastor of the Holiness Church of the Redeemer is probably not going to be too happy about you kissing his daughter.

**LANEY.** She kissed me too.

**ELISE.** Fine. Whatever. I just think you need to give yourself a little more time, before you start making all these declarations, because you see, the Holiness Church of the Redeemer is not going to receive a fourteen-year-old, self-declared lesbian with open arms.

**LANEY.** I'm not self-declared. I just am. I'm a holiness lesbian and nothing is ever going to change that.

**ELISE.** Fine. You're a holiness lesbian.

**LANEY.** I admit, I might meet some resistance, some prejudice. Maybe I'll get thrown out of the church, and Maribel and me will have to move to another town. But when my memoirs are published, other fourteen-year-old holiness lesbians will read them and won't feel so alone.

**ELISE.** Your memoirs?

**LANEY.** Yes. My memoirs.

**ELISE.** Laney, I know you love a good story. And this, it's a good story. But are you sure it's you? Because if it's not you, then you're most likely going to hurt someone.

**LANEY.** I'm gong to put that in my memoirs. I'm going to tell the world that you said that, that you're an unsupportive Mother.

**ELISE.** Go ahead, blame me for everything. That's what I'm here for, to feed your fourteen-year- old delusions. That's what this is, Laney. It's a delusion, and you know, you just can't afford to have delusions, because they run in the family.

**LANEY.** Why do you hate me?

**ELISE.** Laney, I have never given you any reason to think I hate you. You mean more to me than anything in the world. You know that.

**LANEY.** Yes. *(pause)* Why do you hate Maribel?

**ELISE.** Because she's poor and stupid. And a little bit crazy. And because frankly, she's not good enough for you. Not nearly.

## Scene Seven

*(MARIBEL, LANEY and ELISE have just finished eating
dinner. An empty pizza box sits on the floor. ELISE is
drinking a glass of wine, the bottle beside her.)*

**MARIBEL.** My Mom won't let us order pizza.

**ELISE.** No?

**MARIBEL.** She won't let us eat fast food.

**ELISE.** Pizza isn't fast. They say it will be a half-hour, but it
always takes forty five minutes.

**MARIBEL.** My Mom cooks every night. You don't cook every
night.

**ELISE.** No.

**MARIBEL.** Don't you like to cook?

**ELISE.** No, I have never liked to cook.

**MARIBEL.** Did you cook for Laney's Dad?

**ELISE.** No. It's one of the benefits of being a heathen, you
don't have to cook for your husband.

**LANEY.** Mom!

**ELISE.** Peter did the cooking, before he…

**LANEY.** You look very pretty tonight, Maribel. With your
hair pulled back like that. It's very silky and pretty.

**MARIBEL.** Thank you. *(to ELISE)* You grew-up here, right?

**ELISE.** That's right. This was my father's house. He was a
literature professor at the University.

**MARIBEL.** He wrote short stories like Laney?

**ELISE.** No, he wrote long books about short stories.

**LANEY.** Would you like some more sprite, Maribel? I'd be
happy to get you another one.

**MARIBEL.** Okay.

*(LANEY awkwardly kisses MARIBEL on the cheek. MARI-
BEL is unaware and unresponsive. ELISE notices. LANEY
exits.)*

What did Laney's Dad do?

**ELISE.** Peter? Peter was a sociologist at the University of Wisconsin.

**MARIBEL.** What's that?

**ELISE.** Well, a sociologist is someone who studies sociology, you know, the study of how people interact with one another. How they behave in groups, how social institutions operate, that kind of thing.

(**LANEY** *enters with the Sprite.*)

**MARIBEL.** Did you have sex before you got married?

**LANEY.** Gross! You can't ask my Mom about sex.

**MARIBEL.** Why not? My Mom won't ever talk about sex. She didn't even tell me what a period was. I thought I had sat on a razor in the bathtub or something. I couldn't figure out why I was bleeding. I bet Elise told you all about periods when you got yours.

**ELISE.** Laney hasn't…

(**LANEY** *silences* **ELISE** *with a look.*)

I told Laney about periods long before she ever got one.

**LANEY.** Can we please talk about something else?

**ELISE.** I don't know why you're so embarrassed. We're all women here.

**MARIBEL.** Even though you don't know Jesus, Elise, you're much cooler than my Mom.

**ELISE.** Well, thank you, Maribel, I think. You girls can ask me anything, you know. I'm not embarrassed.

**MARIBEL.** Is it true that you can't use tampons until you get married?

**ELISE.** What?

**MARIBEL.** Sister Rebecca told me that unmarried girls have to use pads. She said you can't use tampons until you're married.

**ELISE.** No. That's absolutely false. Using tampons has nothing to do with getting married. It just has to do with comfort and bathing suits.

**MARIBEL.** Did you have sex before you got married?

**ELISE.** Yes.

**MARIBEL.** What did it feel like?

**LANEY.** I thought you weren't ever going to have sex.

**MARIBEL.** I'm not. But since I'm never going to experience it, I want to know what it's like.

**ELISE.** Okay. I'm going to tell you girls the truth about sex, something that no other Mother in the whole state of Mississippi will ever tell you. One…

**LANEY.** Not a list…

**ELISE.** Yes, a list. A sex list. One, don't expect your partner to know how your body works. Learn how your body works yourself and teach your partner if necessary.

**LANEY.** You said you were going to stop being embarrassing!

**ELISE.** I lied. Two, sex feels really good when it's with someone you're not supposed to do it with. It feels great.

**MARIBEL.** Really?

**ELISE.** Yes. Three, that kind of sex feels great. But sex feels most amazing after about ten years of being with someone. When you've gotten over that first phase of bliss, and you've gotten through the onset of disillusionment, and you're finally in this groove of accepting this body beside you for all its flaws, and you've stopped trying to shape it, or bend it to your will, or even looking to it to get you off. When you're just lying there and can accept the body beside you for merely being there beside you, that's when sex can creep up on you and be more wonderful than you ever thought.

**MARIBEL.** You're thinking about Laney's dad, aren't you?

**ELISE.** God, yes.

*(Pause. **LANEY**'s very uncomfortable in this territory. She picks up the pizza box.)*

**LANEY.** I'll take this out.

*(**LANEY** exits. **ELISE** calls after her.)*

**ELISE.** You don't have to.

*(Pause.* **MARIBEL** *and* **ELISE** *are alone.)*

**MARIBEL.** Can I tell you a secret?

**ELISE.** Sure, honey.

**MARIBEL.** I have stigmata.

**ELISE.** What?

**MARIBEL.** I have stigmata. But not the kind where you bleed from your hands and feet. The invisible kind.

**ELISE.** The invisible kind?

**MARIBEL.** Yes. Sometimes I get this pain underneath my skin, and my veins feel like they're going to pop if I don't do something!

**ELISE.** And what do you do when this happens?

**MARIBEL.** I pray.

**ELISE.** Right. I see. *(pause)* You know, it's not uncommon for teenage girls to feel that way.

**MARIBEL.** To have stigmata?

**ELISE.** No, not stigmata. But to feel a kind of invisible pain, you know...a physical manifestation of emotional distress. Sometimes girls hurt themselves, cut themselves, to make the pain visible. Have you ever wanted to do that?

**MARIBEL.** I don't have that. I have stigmata.

**ELISE.** Well, you think you have stigmata.

**MARIBEL.** No, I have it.

**ELISE.** Okay. You have it. But you know, you could talk to someone at school. Maybe a guidance counselor?

**MARIBEL.** About my stigmata?

**ELISE.** Right. *(pause)* Well, you can talk to me. If you get another case of...stigmata, you could call me.

**MARIBEL.** Why?

**ELISE.** Just to check in. Let me know you're okay.

**MARIBEL.** Okay!

**ELISE.** Fine.

*(**LANEY** returns.)*

**LANEY.** What are you talking about?

*(pause)*

**ELISE.** Secrets. Sex secrets.

**LANEY.** Tell me!

**ELISE.** I thought you didn't want me to talk about sex.

**LANEY.** I don't. Because I'm not ever going to have sex. Not with a man.

**ELISE.** Can I hold you to that?

**LANEY.** I'm not.

**ELISE.** We'll see.

**MARIBEL.** At least Laney's kissed a boy. I've never even done that.

**ELISE.** What boy did Laney kiss?

**LANEY.** It's not important.

**MARIBEL.** She kissed a boy named Quentin Compson. At her school in Wisconsin. She told me.

**ELISE.** Quentin Compson?

**MARIBEL.** Yes!

**ELISE.** Laney!

**LANEY.** What?

**ELISE.** You told Maribel you kissed Quentin Compson?

**LANEY.** So?

**ELISE.** Why not David Copperfield? Why not Huck Finn?

**MARIBEL.** I don't get it.

**ELISE.** Come on, Laney, fess up.

**LANEY.** I don't know what you're talking about.

**ELISE.** Maribel, Quentin Compson is a character in *The Sound and the Fury*, a novel by William Faulkner. Laney's never kissed a boy.

**MARIBEL.** Oh. Why did you say… ?

**LANEY.** There was a boy named Quentin Compson in Madison. His parents named him after Quentin Compson in *The Sound and the Fury*.

**ELISE.** Laney!

LANEY. What?

ELISE. Just fess up.

LANEY. You don't know everything I do.

ELISE. But Quentin Compson is a fictional character.

LANEY. I just told you, Quentin in Madison was named after the Faulkner character.

ELISE. But there was no Quentin Compson in Madison!

LANEY. You don't know the name of every boy in Madison.

ELISE. I know that people in Wisconsin do not name their children after characters from Faulkner.

LANEY. Fine, don't believe me.

ELISE. Good, cause I don't.

(pause)

MARIBEL. I failed my driver's test. When the man said to turn on the right blinker I turned on the left. It was so stupid of me.

LANEY. You've told me that story.

MARIBEL. I was telling Elise.

ELISE. That's too bad, honey. I'm sure you can take it again.

MARIBEL. My Dad says I have to wait another year. Keep practicing and all. He sells Mitsubishis but he doesn't make much money off of it, because he doesn't like to fool poor people. He says Jesus wouldn't fool a poor man into over-paying for a Mitsubishi.

ELISE. No, I guess he wouldn't.

MARIBEL. I guess a sociologist wouldn't fool a poor man into over-paying for a Mitsubishi either.

ELISE. Well, Peter wouldn't at least.

MARIBEL. Do you mind talking about him?

ELISE. No. It's fine.

MARIBEL. When did he die?

ELISE. Who?

MARIBEL. Laney's Dad.

ELISE. Laney's Dad is not dead. Laney, did you tell Maribel that your Father was dead?

**LANEY.** No.

**ELISE.** He's not dead.

**LANEY.** I know.

**ELISE.** Why did you think he was, Maribel?

**MARIBEL.** I don't know.

**ELISE.** Did Laney tell you that?

**MARIBEL.** I think so. I don't know.

**ELISE.** Laney?

**LANEY.** I didn't tell her that. She assumed he was dead, and I let her. I didn't lie.

**ELISE.** Peter is not dead. He's severely mentally ill. You hear me, Laney?

**LANEY.** I know! It's not like I don't know that.

**ELISE.** He's institutionalized. He's not dead.

**MARIBEL.** Oh.

　　　*(pause)*

**ELISE.** Maribel, I think it's time I took you home.

**LANEY.** But we were gonna watch movies!

**ELISE.** Not anymore. You can watch movies another time.

**LANEY.** But you said!

**ELISE.** I changed my mind.

**LANEY.** You can't just change your mind.

**ELISE.** Yes, I can. Get your things together, Maribel. I'm going to get my keys, and then we're taking you home.

**LANEY.** Why do you have to always ruin everything!

　　　*(ELISE exits.)*

　　　God! I hate her!

**MARIBEL.** Did you kiss Quentin Compson?

**LANEY.** Yes! God, she doesn't know everything. *(pause)* I don't want you to go.

**MARIBEL.** It's okay.

**LANEY.** I mean it.

(**LANEY** *puts her hand on* **MARIBEL**'s *knee.*)

(**MARIBEL** *stands up quickly.*)

**MARIBEL.** I want to go. I don't feel so good.

**LANEY.** At least let me give you something first.

**MARIBEL.** What is it?

(**LANEY** *takes a folded piece of paper out of her pocket and hands it to* **MARIBEL.**)

**LANEY.** It's a story for you. I'm dedicating it to you.

## Scene Eight

*(LANEY reads the following story to the audience. MARI-BEL sits on the stadium bleachers, reading the story.)*

LANEY. It is a sunny day in June. She wears a yellow dress and sits in a field dotted with dandelions, as white and full as cotton swabs. She picks the flowers and blows on them one by one, beheading them with her sweet breath. Sometimes the wind takes the feathery petals away, but sometimes it brings them back, so her silky black hair is littered with white, like snowflakes. Like dandruff. I sit beside this girl, watching her behead the dandelions one by one, and as the sun sinks into the sky and fireflies come out for the night, I slowly walk my fingers up her creamy, white thigh.

## Scene Nine

*(LANEY approaches MARIBEL sitting on the bleachers.)*

**LANEY.** Hey.

**MARIBEL.** Hi.

**LANEY.** I tried calling you yesterday. Did you get my message?

**MARIBEL.** Uh huh.

**LANEY.** I thought you were going to take me to church.

**MARIBEL.** My Mom didn't feel like driving out to get you.

**LANEY.** Why didn't you call and tell me?

**MARIBEL.** I did. Your phone was busy.

**LANEY.** Maybe we were trying to call one another at the same time. You know, synchronized.

**MARIBEL.** I figured Elise could take you, if you really wanted to come.

**LANEY.** I did want to come.

**MARIBEL.** Why didn't you then?

**LANEY.** I wanted to go with you. Look, I'm sorry I lied about my Dad. You want my dessert?

**MARIBEL.** No. I'm full.

**LANEY.** Well, will you at least look at me?

*(MARIBEL turns around.)*

**MARIBEL.** Sometimes Satan tricks me.

**LANEY.** What?

**MARIBEL.** When I was little, I tried to baptize Gabriel in the bathtub. I wanted to make sure he was saved, even though he was just a baby, so I ran the water in the bathtub, got Gabriel out of his crib and baptized him. He almost drowned, but my Mom came in and pulled him out. Then she laid her hands on me and said, "Satan, I bind you from my daughter, Maribel. Satan, I cast thee out!"

**LANEY.** Why?

**MARIBEL.** Because Satan was tricking me. Made me think I wanted to baptize Gabriel, just so's he could drown.

**LANEY.** I don't believe in Satan.

**MARIBEL.** You're saved now. You have to believe in Satan.

**LANEY.** No. I just believe in Jesus.

**MARIBEL.** I think Satan still tricks me sometimes, confuses me into thinking something's good, when it's really bad.

**LANEY.** Like what?

**MARIBEL.** Like you. Converting you. I think I did it wrong.

**LANEY.** Why?

**MARIBEL.** Because you're acting funny.

**LANEY.** How so?

**MARIBEL.** Your story.

**LANEY.** You didn't like it?

**MARIBEL.** No.

**LANEY.** What didn't you like about it?

**MARIBEL.** You know.

**LANEY.** It's a made-up story. It doesn't mean anything. It's fiction. You know what fiction is, right?

**MARIBEL.** Yes.

**LANEY.** That's all it is. It doesn't have anything to do with my conversion.

**MARIBEL.** You didn't write like that before.

**LANEY.** I was just trying to write in a different genre. You know what a genre is, don't you?

**MARIBEL.** Uh huh.

**LANEY.** What? What is it?

**MARIBEL.** You know.

**LANEY.** Yes, I do. I was just trying to write something different. A romance. My earlier stuff was realism. I wanted to try a romance this time. I didn't mean to freak you out.

**MARIBEL.** I didn't freak out.

**LANEY.** You weren't supposed to take it so realistically. Romance is not realistic.

**MARIBEL.** Oh.

LANEY. That's okay. I forgive you. I know you don't know all that much about writing. Like you don't know about genres and metaphors and stuff cause you're in remedial classes, so it's understandable that you wouldn't get it.

MARIBEL. I got it.

LANEY. No, you didn't.

MARIBEL. I'm not stupid. I got it. The girl in the field with the silky black hair. That's my hair.

LANEY. So?

MARIBEL. So, that story was about me.

LANEY. It wasn't about you. It was inspired by you.

MARIBEL. I don't want to inspire your romance.

LANEY. You and Marcus Grayson.

MARIBEL. Marcus?

LANEY. Yeah. He was the narrator.

MARIBEL. The narrator?

LANEY. Yeah, you know, the person describing the girl in the field. It was inspired by you and Marcus. You know, the story of how he fingered you. But it's not the real story. It's romance.

MARIBEL. But you said "I."

LANEY. So?

MARIBEL. You said, I walk my fingers…you know.

LANEY. So?

MARIBEL. So, I is you.

LANEY. No, it's not. I is the narrator. I is a made-up person. In this case, I is a made-up person inspired by Marcus Grayson. I guess I could see how it might bother you. But nobody knows it was inspired by you and Marcus, and it's not like I can control what inspires me.

MARIBEL. That story was about me…and Marcus?

LANEY. Yeah. You know the thing that happened in the woods. But also, I saw him looking at you.

MARIBEL. You did?

**LANEY.** Yeah, he was looking at you, all admiringly. With longing in his eyes.

**MARIBEL.** He was?

**LANEY.** Yeah. I saw it.

**MARIBEL.** When?

**LANEY.** On Friday. After school, when we were waiting for the buses.

**MARIBEL.** He was looking at me?

**LANEY.** Yeah. With longing in his eyes. Like he was thinking about how you…felt. And that's what inspired me to write the story.

**MARIBEL.** Oh.

**LANEY.** I didn't mean for it to freak you out.

**MARIBEL.** It didn't freak me out.

**LANEY.** You were talking about Satan and drowning and stuff.

**MARIBEL.** It didn't freak me out.

**LANEY.** Talking about Satan is pretty freaky.

**MARIBEL.** You have to believe in Satan if you're going to believe in Jesus.

**LANEY.** How come?

**MARIBEL.** Because if it weren't for Satan, then Jesus wouldn't have had to die on the cross.

**LANEY.** I thought Jesus died for my sins, not for Satan.

**MARIBEL.** Satan is sin. Satan is original sin.

**LANEY.** So my sin comes from Satan. That's cool.

**MARIBEL.** Why?

**LANEY.** Cause that means Satan is responsible for my sins. Blame him.

**MARIBEL.** No, that's not how it works.

**LANEY.** Well then explain it to me, because your religion doesn't make any sense.

**MARIBEL.** It's your religion too.

**LANEY.** I don't believe in Satan.

**MARIBEL.** You have to believe in Satan, if you believe in Jesus.

**LANEY.** Why?

**MARIBEL.** It's hard to explain…

**LANEY.** How am I supposed to believe in something when you can't explain it clearly?

**MARIBEL.** Satan is original sin.

**LANEY.** You've already said that.

**MARIBEL.** Satan makes us do bad things, but you can't just blame him…

**LANEY.** That doesn't make sense!

**MARIBEL.** Satan is…

**LANEY.** I'm waiting…

**MARIBEL.** Satan is…

**LANEY.** Go on…

**MARIBEL.** …a metaphor.

*(This stumps **LANEY**.)*

**LANEY.** For what?

**MARIBEL.** For the harm we've done to God. For the harm we do each other.

## Scene Ten

(**ELISE** *is in the living room, reading the paper.*)

(**LANEY** *enters and sits down on the other side of the room, ignoring her mother. She flips through her notebook.*)

**ELISE.** You want the funnies?

**LANEY.** No.

**ELISE.** You used to find the funnies funny. What are you working on?

**LANEY.** None of your business.

**ELISE.** If it's none of my business, why'd you come downstairs to work on it?

**LANEY.** I'm tired of my room. I need a new creative environment.

**ELISE.** You want to spend time with me.

**LANEY.** No.

**ELISE.** You want to read your new story to me.

**LANEY.** No, I don't. I don't even have a new story. If I had a new story, I wouldn't need a new environment.

**ELISE.** I think you want an audience.

**LANEY.** God! If you're gonna be like that, I'll go.

**ELISE.** You don't have to go.

(**LANEY** *stays.*)

**ELISE.** So how's Maribel?

**LANEY.** She's fine.

**ELISE.** Are you two still an item?

**LANEY.** Yes.

**ELISE.** Still lesbian lovers?

**LANEY.** God!

**ELISE.** Just kidding! I'm kidding. Sit.

**LANEY.** Why do you have to be like that?

**ELISE.** Like what?

**LANEY.** All nice to my friends, like you're a cool Mom or something, and then insult me in front of them.

**ELISE.** I didn't mean to insult you. You shouldn't lie to Maribel all the time.

**LANEY.** You're embarrassing. Talking about sex all the time.

**ELISE.** Well clearly Maribel needs someone to talk about sex with.

**LANEY.** Talking about periods. God. I can't believe you told her I didn't.

**ELISE.** I'm sorry. For that. I shouldn't have said that. But you shouldn't have told Maribel that you kissed Quentin Compson. Christ.

**LANEY.** It's not a big deal. That's the kind of stuff people are supposed to lie about.

**ELISE.** You shouldn't lie about your Dad.

**LANEY.** God! You make me sick.

**ELISE.** What's new?

**LANEY.** I can't believe how you got all weepy over Dad like that, like he was your long lost love or something.

**ELISE.** Your Dad is my long lost love.

**LANEY.** You're divorcing him. He doesn't get to be your long lost love.

**ELISE.** Who says?

**LANEY.** Me. You don't get to be sad.

**ELISE.** Laney, if you haven't noticed, I've been sad. I am sad. I will be sad. Deal with it.

**LANEY.** You don't have any right to be sad. You divorced him.

**ELISE.** I know. I'm a monster.

**LANEY.** You said, till death do you part.

**ELISE.** We did not say till death do you part.

**LANEY.** Yes, you did.

**ELISE.** We got married by a man in an Elvis suit. We didn't say till death do you part.

**LANEY.** But that's what marriage means!

**ELISE.** What would you have me do, Laney, what?

**LANEY.** You shouldn't have sent him away.

**ELISE.** One, is he a harm to himself? Yes. Two, is he a harm to others? Yes. End of story.

**LANEY.** He never hurt me.

**ELISE.** No, he didn't. And do you know why? Because I made sure that he didn't.

**LANEY.** He wouldn't have hurt me.

**ELISE.** Not Peter, no. But the disease very easily could have. Would have. Did.

**LANEY.** I'm fine.

**ELISE.** You're fine?

**LANEY.** Yes.

**ELISE.** Let me list all of the ways you are not fine. One…

**LANEY.** Not your freaking lists!

**ELISE.** You can barely sleep through the night. Two, you can't even stand up straight, because the muscles in your back are in a constant state of tension. Three, you've decided to become a holiness lesbian.

**LANEY.** I knew this was about that…

**ELISE.** Four. You have created a delusional relationship with a grossly immature sixteen year old who thinks she has invisible stigmata!

**LANEY.** She told you?

**ELISE.** Yes, she told me.

**LANEY.** It's not delusional.

**ELISE.** Okay, Laney, okay. You and Maribel are in love. Go write it in your memoirs. The coming of age of a holiness lesbian…

**LANEY.** Don't do that!

**ELISE.** What?

**LANEY.** Don't make fun of me!

**ELISE.** Laney, I've got to take a break. I can't go another round with you today. Can we take a break?

**LANEY.** No!

**ELISE.** What do you want from me?

**LANEY.** Dad understood my writing. He never made fun of me. He said I would win the Nobel Prize for literature someday.

ELISE. That's because Peter was the dreamer. I'm not. I'm the practical one. That's why he was the theorist, and I was in the trenches. That was the difference between us. I'm sorry that you got stuck with the practical one. But that's who I am. I don't believe in giving people false hope. I don't believe in telling lies.

LANEY. You put him in there. You can get him out.

ELISE. Was he a harm to you?

LANEY. No.

ELISE. Did he ever put you in harm?

LANEY. No.

ELISE. Did he ever wake you up in the middle of the night waving a kitchen knife?

LANEY. He was trying to protect me.

ELISE. He thought he was Abraham. He thought you were Isaac.

LANEY. He was trying to protect me!

ELISE. He thought God was telling him to sacrifice his child.

LANEY. He wouldn't have hurt me. Ever.

ELISE. No. But his delusions almost did.

LANEY. You could have tried something else.

ELISE. I tried everything. And then he walked into your bedroom with a knife.

LANEY. You didn't try everything.

ELISE. I did. I tried everything, and then he walked into your bedroom with a knife. Don't you think I want him back? Don't you know that I would have rather lost him to cancer or a car accident, a forest fire, a gas leak, spontaneous combustion, the plague, anything other than this? Do you know how horrible it feels to know that that body, that beautiful body, that laid next to me all those years is in the world, that it's in the world, looking just like him but not him. Something else entirely.

LANEY. You didn't try everything. If you really wanted him back, you would have prayed.

**ELISE.** I would have prayed. Great. To what? To the same God that was telling him to slit your throat?

**LANEY.** If you really wanted him back, you would have prayed to God for him to get better, and he would. But you don't, cause you don't believe in God, because you're too smart to believe in God. So you don't pray, and you haven't tried everything, and so he's sitting there waiting for you in everlasting hell!

**ELISE.** Don't you ever talk to me like that again.

**LANEY.** Why the hell not?

**ELISE.** Because it makes you sound like a crazy person.

## Scene Eleven

(**LANEY** *tries to revise her first story. She speaks to the audience.*)

LANEY. Ernest's hands smelled like gunshot and lemons. No.

They smelled like lemons because he used to eat lemons like oranges. He'd place the fruit in his mouth and peel it with his teeth, while he manned his lemonade stand. No.

Ernest's hands smelled like gunshot and lemons, because he ate the yellow fruit, while cleaning his guns. He'd place the lemons between his teeth and peel off the bitter skin. The...the bitter skin that...that...

Ernest's hands smelled like lemons. He ate the sour fruit like oranges. He'd peel the bitter skin with his teeth and spit it out on the ground. He'd litter his shoes with yellow lemony bits and pieces. At the lemonade stand. At the lemonade stand where the children lined up, they lined up and watched him do it. They watched him do it...They watched...They watched while he pulled out his gun...

Ernest's hands smelled like lemons. They smelled like lemons, because...because...

My father. My father would put a lemon to his mouth and eat it like an orange.

*Scene Twelve*

*(Late at night. In the living room,* **LANEY** *and* **MARIBEL** *have been drinking wine. They hold up their glasses.)*

**LANEY.** I thought the wine was supposed to turn into blood.

**MARIBEL.** Only Catholics think that.

**LANEY.** So you just drink the wine and call it blood?

**MARIBEL.** No, we don't drink wine. We drink grape juice.

**LANEY.** Why do you drink grape juice?

**MARIBEL.** Because drinking alcohol is a sin.

**LANEY.** But Jesus drank wine.

**MARIBEL.** I know. But they didn't have pure water back then.

**LANEY.** What?

**MARIBEL.** The water in Biblical times. It was contaminated. That's why they had to drink wine.

**LANEY.** Where did you hear that?

**MARIBEL.** I don't know.

**LANEY.** Well if Jesus could turn the water into wine, couldn't he just have decontaminated the water?

**MARIBEL.** I don't know. I guess.

**LANEY.** I mean, the fact that Jesus chose to turn the water into wine, rather than just decontaminating it, proves that drinking alcohol is not a sin.

**MARIBEL.** Maybe.

**LANEY.** Here, here.

*(***LANEY*** *takes a big gulp.* ***MARIBEL*** *follows suit.)*

**MARIBEL.** When is Elise coming home?

**LANEY.** I don't know.

**MARIBEL.** You said she'd be here.

**LANEY.** She will be. She had some work thing to go to.

**MARIBEL.** You think she'd let me French twist her hair when she gets back? I think her hair would look good in a French twist.

**LANEY.** Are you like in love with my Mom?

**MARIBEL.** No. I just want to know when she's coming home.

**LANEY.** Later.

*(LANEY pours more wine into MARIBEL's glass. MARIBEL considers the full glass before her.)*

**MARIBEL.** Drunkenness is definitely a sin.

**LANEY.** Then we won't get drunk.

*(LANEY clinks her glass against MARIBEL's and takes a long sip.)*

**MARIBEL.** Laney?

**LANEY.** Yeah?

**MARIBEL.** I think I already am.

**LANEY.** Already what?

**MARIBEL.** Drunk.

**LANEY.** Me too.

*(They erupt into a fit of giggles.)*

**MARIBEL.** You want to know something?

**LANEY.** What?

**MARIBEL.** I'm going to ask Marcus if he wants to go to church with me next week!

**LANEY.** But you said he didn't go anymore.

**MARIBEL.** He doesn't. That's why I'm gonna ask him.

**LANEY.** I don't think that's a good idea.

**MARIBEL.** Why not?

**LANEY.** Well if he wanted to go to church, he would. He already knows about Jesus and everything.

**MARIBEL.** I know.

**LANEY.** So why do you want to ask him?

**MARIBEL.** You know.

**LANEY.** No.

**MARIBEL.** You know.

**LANEY.** No I don't.

**MARIBEL.** You said he was the narrator. You said you saw him looking at me.

**LANEY.** Oh.

**MARIBEL.** With longing in his eyes. I think he wants me to ask him. I'm going to do it. Monday, after school.

*(pause)*

**LANEY.** I don't think you should.

**MARIBEL.** Why not?

**LANEY.** Well, I might've been wrong.

**MARIBEL.** What do you mean?

**LANEY.** I might've been wrong about him looking at you like that. I mean, he was looking at you and everything, but there might not have been longing in his eyes.

**MARIBEL.** But you said…

**LANEY.** I know. That's what I thought at the time, but now that I think about it again, I could've been wrong.

**MARIBEL.** Were you lying again?

**LANEY.** No! I wasn't lying. But you know it's really hard to know what people are thinking sometimes. They might be thinking one thing, but look like they're thinking something else. Like maybe Marcus wasn't looking at you with longing in his eyes. Maybe he was looking at a girl standing behind you.

**MARIBEL.** Was there a girl standing behind me?

**LANEY.** I don't know. Maybe. I can't remember. *(pause)* Don't get upset! I don't think there was a girl behind you. I really do think he was looking at you all longingly, but just in case, maybe you shouldn't ask him to church right away. Just give him some time. Let him make the first move.

**MARIBEL.** You think he will?

**LANEY.** I think he definitely might.

*(**MARIBEL** slowly smiles. They clink glasses again and drink. **ELISE** enters.)*

**ELISE.** What's going on here?

*(**LANEY** and **MARIBEL** try to hide their glasses.)*

**LANEY.** Nothing.

**ELISE.** Nothing? Having a cocktail party are you?

**MARIBEL.** We were just taking communion.

**ELISE.** Communion?

**MARIBEL.** Uh huh.

**LANEY.** We just wanted to see what it tasted like.

**MARIBEL.** Laney said that since Jesus chose to turn the water into wine instead of decontaminating the water, then drinking alcohol isn't a sin.

**ELISE.** Laney said that?

**MARIBEL.** Uh huh.

**ELISE.** Maribel, you shouldn't believe everything Laney says. Haven't you learned that by now? To bed. Both of you. Right now.

*(pause)*

**LANEY.** Okay, but we have to say our prayers first. Maribel?

**MARIBEL.** Yeah?

**LANEY.** We have to say a prayer.

**ELISE.** Laney, stop it.

**LANEY.** You know a prayer, right?

**MARIBEL.** I know lots of prayers.

**LANEY.** Then say one.

**ELISE.** I said to bed!

*(MARIBEL and LANEY kneel.)*

**MARIBEL.** Now I lay me down to sleep,
I pray the Lord my soul to sheep.
I said sheep.

*(MARIBEL erupts with laughter.)*

**ELISE.** *(to LANEY)* Why are you doing this?

**LANEY.** I'm not doing anything.

**ELISE.** You're doing this intentionally.

**LANEY.** What?

**ELISE.** Making me crazy!

**LANEY.** I can't make someone crazy. Either they're crazy, or they're not.

**ELISE.** You know what I mean.

**LANEY.** Maribel, finish your prayer.

**MARIBEL.** Okay. The Lord is my shepherd I do not want. He maketh me to sheep in green pastures.

*(She can't stop giggling.)*

**ELISE.** Alright. Prayers are finished. To bed.

**LANEY.** That's not the end of the prayer. Is that the end of the prayer, Maribel?

**MARIBEL.** No.

**LANEY.** It's not the end of the prayer.

**ELISE.** You are on thin ice, young lady.

**LANEY.** Finish the prayer, Maribel. And then we'll go to bed.

**ELISE.** Fine. Finish the prayer, and then you'll go to bed, and then you'll be grounded for a month.

**LANEY.** Fine. Maribel?

**MARIBEL.** Lo, though I walk through the pasture of death. I feed no evil, for thou art with me…

**LANEY.** For thou art with me.

**MARIBEL.** I feed no evil. No evil is fed by me.

**LANEY.** No evil is fed by me. Thank you, Jesus.

**ELISE.** Stop it, Laney.

**LANEY.** *(to* **MARIBEL***)* Go on.

**MARIBEL.** At the table of my enemies, you feed us sheep.

**LANEY.** You feed us sheep!

**ELISE.** That's enough.

**MARIBEL.** You feed the sheep us.

**LANEY.** You said we could finish the prayer.

**MARIBEL.** Us, the sheep, you feed!

**ELISE.** Maribel, will you please shut-up!

**LANEY.** You can't tell my friend to shut-up!

**ELISE.** God-damnit, Laney! I've had enough of you. All this stops right now. All the histrionics and hissy fits. All the hand-raising and praising out to the Lord. It stops right now.

LANEY. You can't make me stop believing in God. You can't control my mind like that.

ELISE. I'm not trying to control your mind, but I am putting a stop to all of this.

LANEY. All of what?

ELISE. All of your drama! All of your lying and lesbianism and bedtime prayers. It stops right now.

LANEY. You can't stop who I am.

ELISE. I'm not trying to stop who you are, but I am going to make you be honest with yourself. With everyone.

MARIBEL. You're a lesbian?

LANEY. No. No, I'm not.

ELISE. But you told me that you were a holiness lesbian. That's what you said, isn't it?

MARIBEL. A holiness lesbian?

LANEY. That's not true.

ELISE. Were you lying?

LANEY. No.

ELISE. Well, are you lying now?

LANEY. No.

ELISE. Which is it, Laney? Were you lying to me earlier, or are you lying to Maribel now?

*(pause)*

LANEY. Maribel, my Mom thinks you're poor and stupid and crazy.

MARIBEL. You do?

ELISE. Laney!

MARIBEL. You said that about me?

LANEY. Yes. My Mom thinks you're stupid and crazy and that your religion is a pile of shit.

ELISE. Laney, shut your mouth!

MARIBEL. You think that?

ELISE. No.

LANEY. Yes, you do. Don't lie.

**ELISE.** I'm not lying. You are way out of control, young lady.

**LANEY.** You said it.

**ELISE.** I never said your religion was a pile of shit, Maribel.

**LANEY.** You said she was stupid and crazy. Don't lie.

**MARIBEL.** Did you say that?

**ELISE.** No.

**LANEY.** Don't lie!

**ELISE.** I said, I said…I just don't agree with your beliefs, that's all.

**LANEY.** She thinks you're a bad influence on me.

**ELISE.** I thought that at first. But I don't think so anymore.

**MARIBEL.** You think I'm a bad influence?

**LANEY.** Tell her she's stupid!

**ELISE.** No!

**LANEY.** That's what she said about you, Maribel. She said you're stupid. And fat. And lazy.

**ELISE.** Maribel, I never said any of those things…

**LANEY.** She thinks you're grossly immature. She thinks you're borderline retarded!

**ELISE.** Shut your mouth!

**LANEY.** She said if you were her daughter, she'd divorce you! She said she'd lock you in the attic, where you would grow old and mad and humpbacked and alone forever. That's what they do to people like us. They lock us in attics so no one ever has to see us or talk to us or look at us ever again. Look at how disgusting we are! Look at me! Look at me and tell me how disgusting I am, how disgusting and humpbacked and mad, mad, mad I'll always be! Tell me!

**ELISE.** Laney, baby…

**LANEY.** Say it.

**ELISE.** No.

**LANEY.** Say it!

**ELISE.** No. How can you think that?

LANEY. How could I not? This is what I see. Maribel, you disgust me.

*(LANEY runs out of the room to another section of the house, perhaps to her room or the front porch. ELISE looks down at MARIBEL sitting on the floor, crying and shaking. She hesitates for a brief moment, then chooses to run after her daughter.)*

*(Split scene. Lights remain on MARIBEL in the living room, deeply distressed. She rubs her palms together, trying to get rid of the pain. She rubs her hands against the floor, the sofa, anything to get rid of the pain. Shaking, she lifts her hands upwards to release the pain, but it does not work.)*

ELISE. Laney, baby. You are none of those things to me. You are none of those things period.

LANEY. This is what I see.

ELISE. Look at me. We are just having a rough time right now, but you are none of those things to me.

LANEY. But that's what you really think, isn't it? You think I'm unrealistic. You think I'm delusional! You think I'm gonna end up like Dad.

ELISE. No, you are dead wrong.

LANEY. Don't lie.

ELISE. I don't think that.

LANEY. Don't lie to me!

ELISE. Okay. Listen to me. Sometimes I'm afraid you might inherit your father's illness. But you know what, Laney, that's all it is. Fear. Stupid, insidious fear. And I'm so sorry I let it creep into this house. I'm so very sorry, because where I truly see your father in you is in your creativity. In your brilliance. I believe you are going to accomplish great things. But I can't promise everything is going to be okay in twenty years or even tomorrow. The truth is terrible things have happened to us. Terrible things will come again. We can't know what they will be. The only thing I can promise you is that there is nothing, nothing, nothing in the world that would ever make me leave you.

**LANEY.** How do you know?

**ELISE.** Because I'm your mother.

**LANEY.** No. How can you really know?

*(Lights up on* **MARIBEL***, still shaking and crying, the pain unbearable. She picks up the wine corkscrew from the floor.)*

**ELISE.** Because...I have a love for you that surpasses all understanding.

*(***MARIBEL*** impales her hand with the corkscrew. The blood flows. A wave of relief.)*

*(Mother and daughter embrace.* **MARIBEL** *remains on the floor, bleeding and alone.)*

*(Light go down.)*

### The End

## PROPERTY LIST

Notebook
Pen or pencil
2 Lunch bags with food items (optional)
Backpack
Messenger bag
Various textbooks and binders (optional)
Bag of groceries with carton of cigarettes
4 Sprite Cans
2 Flashlights
Cake
4 Wine glasses
2 Bottles of wine
Wine substitute
Empty pizza box
Folded piece of paper
Sunday paper
Corkscrew
Stage blood

# From the Reviews of
# **CROOKED...**

**Also by**
**Catherine Trieschmann...**

# The Bridegroom
# of Blowing Rock

Please visit our website **samuelfrench.com** for complete
descriptions and licensing information

# OTHER TITLES AVAILABLE FROM SAMUEL FRENCH

## CAPTIVE
Jan Buttram

*Comedy / 2m, 1f / Interior*

A hilarious take on a father/daughter relationship, this off beat comedy combines foreign intrigue with down home philosophy. Sally Pound flees a bad marriage in New York and arrives at her parent's home in Texas hoping to borrow money from her brother to pay a debt to gangsters incurred by her husband. Her elderly parents are supposed to be vacationing in Israel, but she is greeted with a shotgun aimed by her irascible father who has been left home because of a minor car accident and is not at all happy to see her. When a news report indicates that Sally's mother may have been taken captive in the Middle East, Sally's hard-nosed brother insists that she keep father home until they receive definite word, and only then will he loan Sally the money. Sally fails to keep father in the dark, and he plans a rescue while she finds she is increasingly unable to skirt the painful truths of her life. The ornery father and his loveable but slightly-dysfunctional daughter come to a meeting of hearts and minds and solve both their problems.

# SAMUEL FRENCH STAFF

**Nate Collins**
President

**Ken Dingledine**
Director of Operations,
Vice President

**Bruce Lazarus**
Executive Director,
General Counsel

**Rita Maté**
Director of Finance

### ACCOUNTING

**Lori Thimsen** | Director of Licensing Compliance
**Nehal Kumar** | Senior Accounting Associate
**Josephine Messina** | Accounts Payable
**Helena Mezzina** | Royalty Administration
**Joe Garner** | Royalty Administration
**Jessica Zheng** | Accounts Receivable
**Andy Lian** | Accounts Receivable
**Zoe Qiu** | Accounts Receivable
**Charlie Sou** | Accounting Associate
**Joann Mannello** | Orders Administrator

### BUSINESS AFFAIRS

**Lysna Marzani** | Director of Business Affairs
**Kathryn McCumber** | Business Administrator

### CUSTOMER SERVICE AND LICENSING

**Brad Lohrenz** | Director of Licensing Development
**Fred Schnitzer** | Business Development Manager
**Laura Lindson** | Licensing Services Manager
**Kim Rogers** | Professional Licensing Associate
**Matthew Akers** | Amateur Licensing Associate
**Ashley Byrne** | Amateur Licensing Associate
**Glenn Halcomb** | Amateur Licensing Associate
**Derek Hassler** | Amateur Licensing Associate
**Jennifer Carter** | Amateur Licensing Associate
**Kelly McCready** | Amateur Licensing Associate
**Annette Storckman** | Amateur Licensing Associate
**Chris Lonstrup** | Outgoing Information Specialist

### EDITORIAL AND PUBLICATIONS

**Amy Rose Marsh** | Literary Manager
**Ben Coleman** | Editorial Associate
**Gene Sweeney** | Graphic Designer
**David Geer** | Publications Supervisor
**Charlyn Brea** | Publications Associate
**Tyler Mullen** | Publications Associate

### MARKETING

**Abbie Van Nostrand** | Director of Corporate
Communications
**Ryan Pointer** | Marketing Manager
**Courtney Kochuba** | Marketing Associate

### OPERATIONS

**Joe Ferreira** | Product Development Manager
**Casey McLain** | Operations Supervisor
**Danielle Heckman** | Office Coordinator, Reception

### SAMUEL FRENCH BOOKSHOP (LOS ANGELES)

**Joyce Mehess** | Bookstore Manager
**Cory DeLair** | Bookstore Buyer
**Jennifer Palumbo** | Customer Service Associate
**Sonya Wallace** | Bookstore Associate
**Tim Coultas** | Bookstore Associate
**Monté Patterson** | Bookstore Associate
**Robin Hushbeck** | Bookstore Associate
**Alfred Contreras** | Shipping & Receiving

### LONDON OFFICE

**Felicity Barks** | Rights & Contracts Associate
**Steve Blacker** | Bookshop Associate
**David Bray** | Customer Services Associate
**Zena Choi** | Professional Licensing Associate
**Robert Cooke** | Assistant Buyer
**Stephanie Dawson** | Amateur Licensing Associate
**Simon Ellison** | Retail Sales Manager
**Jason Felix** | Royalty Administration
**Susan Griffiths** | Amateur Licensing Associate
**Robert Hamilton** | Amateur Licensing Associate
**Lucy Hume** | Publications Manager
**Nasir Khan** | Management Accountant
**Simon Magniti** | Royalty Administration
**Louise Mappley** | Amateur Licensing Associate
**James Nicolau** | Despatch Associate
**Martin Phillips** | Librarian
**Zubayed Rahman** | Despatch Associate
**Steve Sanderson** | Royalty Administration Supervisor
**Douglas Schatz** | Acting Executive Director
**Roger Sheppard** | I.T. Manager
**Geoffrey Skinner** | Company Accountant
**Peter Smith** | Amateur Licensing Associate
**Garry Spratley** | Customer Service Manager
**David Webster** | UK Operations Director

# GET THE NAME OF YOUR CAST AND CREW IN PRINT WITH SPECIAL EDITIONS!

Special Editions are a unique, fun way to commemorate your production and RAISE MONEY.

The Samuel French Special Edition is a customized script personalized to *your* production. Your cast and crew list, photos from your production and special thanks will all appear in a Samuel French Acting Edition alongside the original text of the play.

These Special Editions are powerful fundraising tools that can be sold in your lobby or throughout your community in advance.

These books have autograph pages that make them perfect for year book memories, or gifts for relatives unable to attend the show. Family and friends will cherish this one of a kind souvenier.

Everyone will want a copy of these beautiful, personalized scripts!

ORDER YOUR COPIES TODAY!
E-MAIL SPECIALEDITIONS@SAMUELFRENCH.COM
OR CALL US AT 1-866-598-8449!